MW01142190

For Téo and Max.
For Noélie, Cléo and Franck.

Coo's
in love

Text by Karine Laurent
Illustrations by Stéphanie Alastra

AUZOU

CHICKEN STORAGE

Coo the hen, lived peacefully on Lay'n Egg Farm.
Coo was the farmyard dressmaker.
Her reputation was well-established and
she stood head and shoulders above everyone else!
But Coo had a secret that she kept all to herself.

Coo was deeply in love with a magnificent carrier pigeon, Flyflatout, who would stop off at the chicken coop after each of his trips.

100% top
quality chicken

But Coo was convinced that she would never be able to catch his eye.
She was too shy.
And what's more, she thought she was too small and much too plump!

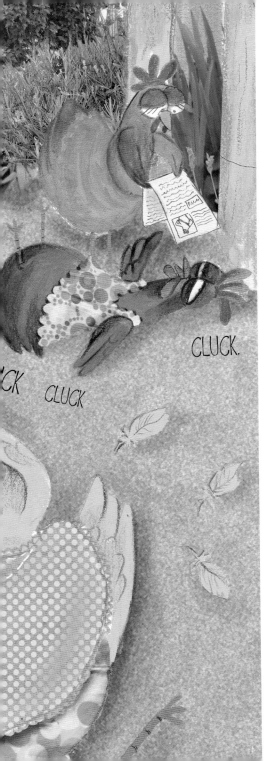

One evening, a poster announcing the impending arrival of Flyflatout created an incredible stir at the farm. All the young chicks were in a tizzy!

"Flyflatout is coming back," said Little Feather.

"Cluck, cluck, cluck! I have to get myself ready", exclaimed Cluckie.

"Flyflatout, the Pigeon with the finest plumage will be here soon!"

Coo found herself with a huge amount of sewing on her wings, for each chick wanted to be prettier than the others. A crest here, three feathers there and stitch, stitch, stitch...
She worked around the clock!

When Flyflatout arrived, all the chickens were dressed to the nines.
Only Coo, owing to lack of time, was not ready.

Faced with so many rivals, Coo promised herself
that she would soon be the most beautiful of them all.
"You'll see, my pretty ones, I've got a brilliant idea!
That pigeon won't be able to ignore me any longer, I'm sure!"
She began to sew day and night.

Coo had made herself
a magnificent...
turtledove dress!
Stylish and elegant, she
thought she looked perfect!

Thinking she was alone, Coo started strutting up and down in her new costume, when someone landed behind her.
"Well, my little chicken," said Flyflatout "what are you doing here all alone?
How on earth did he recognize me?"
Coo wondered in surprise.

"You're mistaken, Sir, my name is Lilibelle
the Turtledove."

Flyflatout Pigeon succumbed to her charm immediately.
"Dear Lilibelle the Turtledove, I must leave this evening
but I'll be back in three days and I would like
to see you again."

Coo, the little chicken-turtledove, blinked
and lowered her head.
"Oh! Ah... yes!

Finally, the evening she had so eagerly awaited arrived.
Coo climbed onto the roof of the chicken coop to put on her turtledove costume and wait for her loved one.

Flyflatout arrived, landing lightly and elegantly.

"I have a proposal for you, my dear Lilibelle,"
he said, offering her a gold ring.
"Let's go away and discover the world. Let's fly away
and love each other!"
Poor Lilibelle was undone- chickens could not fly!
Even her beautiful costume would not change that.
"Let's wait a day or two," the turtledove replied,
feeling very sad that she was only a hen.

Coo made a few unsucceddful attempts to fly.
She ended up bruised all over.
"Why did I lie to him?" she wept. "I'm ridiculous,
but I'm so terribly in love!"

Two days later, Coo slipped on her turtledove costume and went
to wait for Flyflatout on the roof of the chicken coop.
The pigeon landed delicately after flying in big heart-shaped patterns
above his loved one.

When Flyflatout put his wing around Lilibelle's neck,
she suddenly had a bout of hiccups and lost her balance.

She tumbled heavily to the ground, tearing her costume as she fell!

When Flyflatout discovered the truth, he flew off without even
a backwards glance at Coo, the poor ashamed chicken.
The pigeon did not reappear in the coming days,

and so sad little Coo resumed her sewing activities.

One evening, around bedtime, the door of the chicken coop flew open. Without a word, Flyflatout strode up to Coo and handed her a big long parcel.

Nervously, she opened it.
"Oh, a pair of made-to-measure turtledove wings signed
by Blédor, the famous fashion designer for feathered creatures!
"They're magnificent!" Coo gasped.
"Listen, dear Coo, never mind our differences; said Flyflatout
"what matters is... I love you!

Coo put on her wings and, with her heart beating fast, approached the edge of the gutter. Flyflatout encouraged her.
"Go on, my sweetheart, fly with your own wings! Let's leave, my love."

With these words, Coo unfolded her wings and let herself slip
off the roof.

With a few flaps of her wings, she rose into the sky next to her loved one and together, they flew away, wing in wing.

At Lay'n Egg Farm, it is even said that they have flown around the world three times!

General Management: Gauthier Auzou
Editing: Florence Pierron
Layout: Studio Auzou
Production: Brigitte Trichet
Rereading: Gwenaëlle Hamon, Fanny Letournel
Photoengraver: Turquoise

© Éditions Philippe Auzou, Paris - France, 2009

All rights reserved. No part of this book may be used or reproduced
in any form or by any means, electronic or mechanical, including
photocopying, recording, or by any information storage and retrieval
system, without permission in writing from the publisher.

❦ Printed and bound in China

ISBN: 978-2733-812440

In the same collection

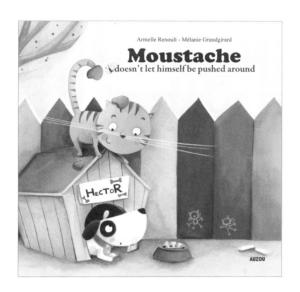

Armelle Renoult - Mélanie Grandgirard

Moustache
doesn't let himself be pushed around

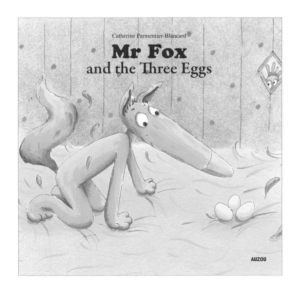

Catherine Parmentier-Blancard

Mr Fox
and the Three Eggs

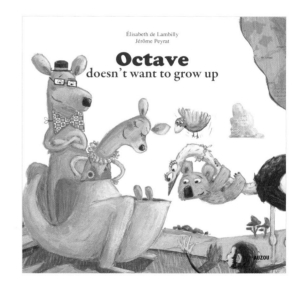

Élisabeth de Lambilly
Jérôme Peyrat

Octave
doesn't want to grow up

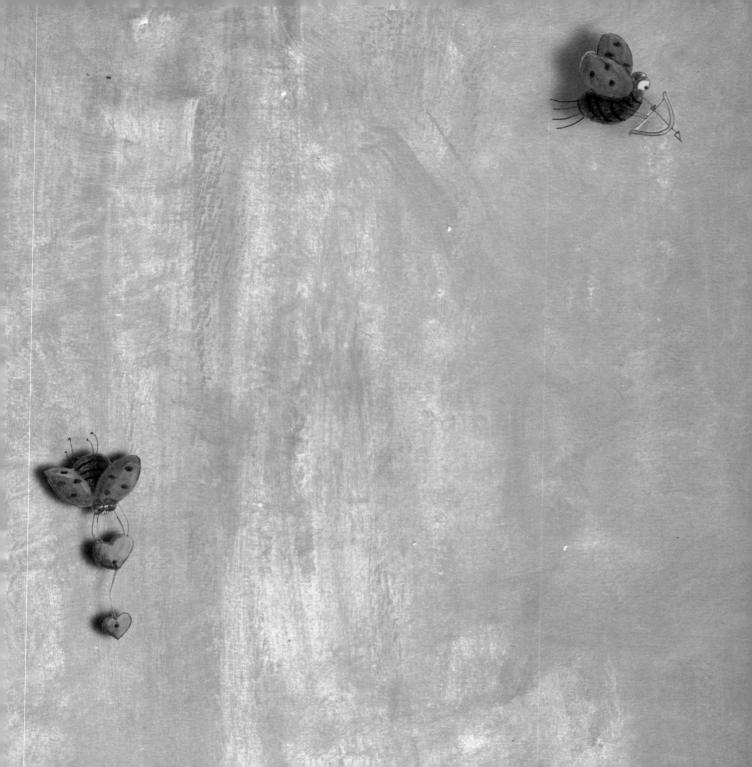